A Note from Michelle about
How to Be Cool

Hi! I'm Michelle Tanner. I'm nine years old. And you won't believe what the kids at school wrote about me in their slam book. They all think I'm boring!

But wait—it gets worse. I found out my whole family thinks I'm boring too. And I have a *big* family.

There's my dad and my two older sisters, D.J. and Stephanie. But that's not all.

My mom died when I was little. So my uncle Jesse moved in to help Dad take care of us. So did Joey Gladstone. He's my dad's friend from college. It's almost like having three dads. But that's still not all!

First Uncle Jesse got married to Becky Donaldson. Then they had twin boys, Nicky and Alex. The twins are four years old now. And they're so cute.

That's nine people. Our dog, Comet, makes ten.

And I have to show them all that I'm not boring. I'm going to prove that I know how to be cool.

FULL HOUSE™ MICHELLE novels

The Great Pet Project
The Super-Duper Sleepover Party
My Two Best Friends
Lucky, Lucky Day
The Ghost in My Closet
Ballet Surprise
Major League Trouble
My Fourth-Grade Mess
Bunk 3, Teddy and Me
My Best Friend Is a Movie Star!
The Big Turkey Escape
The Substitute Teacher
Calling All Planets
I've Got a Secret
How to Be Cool

Available from MINSTREL Books

FULL HOUSE™
Michelle

How to Be Cool

Suzanne Weyn

A Parachute Press Book

Published by POCKET BOOKS
New York   London   Toronto   Sydney   Tokyo   Singapore

A MINSTREL PAPERBACK *Original*

 A Minstrel Book published by
POCKET BOOKS, a division of Simon & Schuster Inc.
1230 Avenue of the Americas, New York, NY 10020

A PARACHUTE PRESS BOOK

 Copyright © and ™ 1997 by Warner Bros.

FULL HOUSE, characters, names and all related indicia are trademarks of Warner Bros. © 1997.

ISBN: 0-671-00833-1

First Minstrel Books printing July 1997

10 9 8 7 6 5 4 3 2 1

A MINSTREL BOOK and colophon are registered trademarks of Simon & Schuster Inc.

Cover photo by Schultz Photography

Printed in the U.S.A.

How to Be Cool

Chapter

1

♥ "Michelle, have you seen the slam book yet?" Kelly Middleton whispered.

Michelle shook her head. Kelly slid a green-and-blue notebook onto Michelle's desk. The words "slam book" were printed across the front in big red letters.

Michelle glanced up. Mrs. Yoshida's back was to the class as she wrote a math problem on the board.

Her teacher didn't like slam books. Mrs. Yoshida didn't allow them in her class. She thought if you had something to say about someone, you should say it to their face—

not write it in a notebook without even signing your name.

I'd better wait until after class to read this, Michelle thought. She slid the book inside her desk.

But I can't wait, she thought. I have to see what everyone wrote about me.

She slid the book back out again.

Michelle placed the book in her lap and started flipping through the pages. There was one page for each kid.

She decided to go back and write something on each page later. Right now she had to read what they wrote about *her*.

Michelle is nice. That was the first note on her page. Someone else wrote: *A good kid.*

Michelle pushed her strawberry-blond bangs off her forehead. Not bad, she thought.

Michelle is a great friend, a great softball captain, and just great! I know who wrote

2

that one, Michelle thought. Cassie! She recognized her best friend's handwriting.

Her other best friend, Mandy, wrote: *Michelle is the best!* She had decorated her note with a circle of hearts and stars—she always did that. Michelle smiled.

I'm going to have to come up with something special for Cassie's and Mandy's slam book pages, Michelle thought.

She kept reading. *A good speler. I mean spehler. No, speller!*

Oh, man! A good speller? Michelle thought. I *am* a good speller—but is that all someone could think to write about me?

Michelle needs a sun hat so she won't get any Tanner. Michelle snorted. That one was kind of funny. Dumb—but funny. She bet her friend Jeff Farrington wrote it. He was always joking around.

The next line read: *Kind of quiet.*

That isn't true! She always answers questions in class. She spends every lunch

3

period and recess talking to her friends. Who thought she was quiet?

Michelle stared around the room, trying to figure it out. But she couldn't.

She read the next comment in the slam book. *Not much.*

What did that mean anyway? It sounded horrible. *Not much.*

Michelle started to shut the notebook. Then she noticed Loreen West's page. Wow! Michelle couldn't believe what the kids wrote about her! *Loreen rules! Loreen is an original, so cool. Loreen is awesome and amazing! I want to be Loreen.*

Whoa! Michelle wished kids had written exciting stuff like that on her page.

But, no. Her page said: *Not much. Quiet. Good kid. Nice. A good speller.*

Compared to Loreen's notes, Michelle's sounded so boring. Boring! Boring! Boring!

Oh, no! Is that what all this means? Michelle thought. Do the kids in my class think I'm *boring?*

And think Loreen is cool.

Michelle glanced over at Loreen. She had short, spiky hair. She wore oversized clothes and big earrings.

Loreen didn't just look cool. She had an amazing singing voice. She was going to sing in the school talent show next month. Spike Henderson and Brian Oakley, two other super-cool fourth-grade kids, were playing backup for her.

"Are you with us, Michelle?" Mrs. Yoshida called.

Michelle jerked her head up. Mrs. Yoshida smiled at her from the front of the classroom.

"Oh, sorry. I'm here," Michelle apologized. The class giggled.

"We can see that," Mrs. Yoshida joked.

The class laughed again. Michelle felt herself blush.

"What were you thinking about so hard? I called your name three times," Mrs. Yoshida said.

I can't tell her I was sitting here wondering if I'm boring! That would be too embarrassing.

"I was wondering if I was . . . uh . . . forgetting something. You know, some homework or something?" Michelle said.

"Well, are you?"

"Am I what?" Michelle asked.

"Forgetting something," Mrs. Yoshida answered.

"Oh! I don't know," Michelle confessed. "I guess I forgot if I forgot."

The class laughed again. But this time they were laughing at her little joke. It made her feel better.

Mrs. Yoshida returned to the math lesson. Michelle slid the slam book into her backpack and tried to concentrate. But all she could think about was whether or not she was boring.

Finally she decided she was. If she wasn't boring, there would have been great stuff written about her in the slam book—like the notes on Loreen West's page.

I'm boring. The thought repeated itself in her head again and again as Mrs. Yoshida moved from math to social studies.

I'm boring. I'm boring. I'm boooring!

When the lunch bell rang, Michelle jumped out of her chair. She needed to talk to her two best friends—right away! She grabbed her backpack and met Cassie and Mandy at the front of the classroom.

"What's with you today?" Mandy asked as they headed to the cafeteria. "You were staring out the window all through social studies!"

"Yeah. What's up?" Cassie asked.

Michelle looked around to make sure no one was listening. "Do you think I'm boring?" she asked.

"What are you talking about?" Cassie exclaimed.

"No way!" Mandy cried.

Michelle pulled the slam book from her backpack and showed them her page.

"Nice doesn't mean *boring,"* Mandy said. "Just forget about it."

"But look at Loreen's page," Michelle insisted. "That's what I want *my* page to be like."

"Michelle, you have tons of friends. If you were really boring, you wouldn't have any!" Cassie said.

"Yeah, everyone thinks you're great," Mandy said.

"If they thought that, they would have written that I was awesome and amazing," Michelle answered.

Then she started to smile. "But there's still time. . . ."

"Time for what?" Cassie asked.

"Um, you'll see," Michelle said thoughtfully.

Michelle couldn't wait to get home that afternoon. She had a great idea! A lot of kids hadn't signed the slam book yet. So all she had to do was keep it in her backpack.

I won't let anyone else write in the slam book until I can make myself as cool as Loreen, she thought. Or even cooler!

People will write great stuff about the cool new me—and I'll have the best slam-book page ever!

Chapter 2

 Michelle opened her bedroom closet. She let out a long sigh. "These are the clothes of a totally boring person," she said.

"Talking to yourself, Michelle?" Michelle's thirteen-year-old sister, Stephanie, strolled into their room.

Michelle didn't answer.

"Earth to Michelle," Stephanie said. "Have you seen my backpack? I'm going over to Darcy's, and I need it."

Michelle still didn't answer. She kept staring into the closet. She was looking for a cool outfit.

Stephanie tiptoed up behind Michelle. She brought her lips close to Michelle's ear. "Hellooo in there," she called.

"My clothes stink," Michelle wailed.

Stephanie laughed. "No, they don't. You're just tired of them," she said. She turned around and grabbed a couple of magazines off her night table—*Classy* and *Young Sass.*

"Why don't you go through these?" Stephanie suggested. She handed the magazines to Michelle. "You might get some ideas. Sometimes all you need is a different belt, or something simple like that, to make your clothes seem new again."

Stephanie found her backpack and headed for the door. "Good luck!" she called as she ran down the stairs.

"Thanks," Michelle yelled back. Then she stretched out on her bed to read *Classy.* Maybe Stephanie was right. Maybe she could find a way to snazz up her clothes or find a great new look in the magazines!

Hmmm, Michelle thought when she found a fashion article called "Say It with Flowers." Everything the models wore had flowers on them. Flowered skirts and flowered dresses. Hats with little fake flowers. Even shoes with daisies on the toes.

Definitely not what I'm looking for. Michelle shook her head.

She flipped a few more pages and found an article called "Bring Back the Bell-bottoms."

Michelle stared at the wide-bottomed pants. She thought they looked funny—not cool.

I hope there is something better in here, Michelle thought. She flipped through the pages faster and faster.

Then she spotted an article called "The Girls of Rock 'n' Roll." Yes! The models were so cool-looking. They made Michelle want to look just like them.

At the end of the article was a section called "A Rockin' Makeover." It showed exactly how to create the clothes the models had on.

"Perfect," Michelle said out loud. "Exactly what I need!"

She read the instructions carefully. Then she pulled her favorite long-sleeved T-shirt out of her closet.

She took out a pair of scissors from her art box.

She gazed from the shirt to the scissors and grinned.

Snip! Snip! Snip!

Coolness, here I come!

Chapter

3

♥ "Michelle! What happened to your clothes?" her father cried.

Michelle twirled around in front of the couch where her dad and Joey Gladstone were sitting. Joey was Danny's best friend. He'd lived with the Tanners since Michelle's mother died.

"Pretty amazing, huh?" she asked them. Michelle loved the way her clothes turned out. She'd made fringes on the hem of her shirt and cut a bigger neckline. Then she'd cut little diamonds in the sleeves.

Well, all of them didn't look *exactly* like

diamonds, Michelle thought. But they were close enough. And at least no one would call her shirt *boring*.

She'd cut holes in the knees of her jeans so they would go with her shirt.

"Well?" Michelle asked. She held her arms out to her sides. "What do you think?"

"Uh, you did that to your clothes on purpose?" her dad asked.

"Of course not," Joey said. "She was attacked by clothes-eating moths from outer space!"

Joey was a professional comedian, but Michelle didn't think his joke was too funny.

Before she could answer, Uncle Jesse came through the swinging kitchen door. He stared hard at Michelle. "Interesting look," he said.

When Michelle's mother died, Uncle Jesse moved in with them too. Now he was married. He and his wife, Aunt Becky, and their four-year-old twins, Nicky and Alex, lived on the third floor.

Michelle could tell from the expression on Uncle Jesse's face that he didn't really like her outfit either.

What was wrong with everyone? Michelle thought the girl in the *Classy* article looked great. Totally cool. And she thought she did too.

"Michelle, those clothes were practically new. If you want to experiment, do it on your old clothes, please," Danny said. "And discuss it with me first."

"But, Dad—" Michelle began to protest.

The front door swung open, and her eighteen-year-old sister, D.J., hurried in. She froze when she saw Michelle. "Whoa," she muttered.

"You like my outfit, don't you?" Michelle asked D.J. "I just finished making it. It took me only about an hour."

D.J. folded her arms and studied Michelle. "Well . . . it's . . . different."

Michelle frowned. "You hate it."

"No, not exactly," D.J. said. "I have to get used to it. It doesn't seem to be . . . you."

"That's great!" Michelle smiled. "I don't want to be me."

"Who *do* you want to be?" Danny asked.

"Me . . . but different. Cooler."

"Now I understand!" Joey laughed. "You cut your clothes up to let in some air. Now you're *cooler*."

Michelle shook her head. Another dumb joke!

Aunt Becky came in from the kitchen. Her thick brown hair bounced around her shoulders as she looked around. "What's going on? Family meeting?" she asked.

"Michelle wants to change her image," Danny told her, shoving his fingers through his hair. "She thinks she needs to be cooler."

Aunt Becky cocked her head to one side as she gazed at Michelle. "I see."

Maybe Aunt Becky will understand, Michelle thought. At least she didn't make jokes or frown or look confused.

Aunt Becky put her hands on her hips. "Everyone start getting ready for dinner. I want to talk to Michelle for a minute."

The family headed for the kitchen. Aunt Becky sat on the couch. Michelle plopped down next to her.

"I think it's terrific you want a new look," Aunt Becky said. "I like to have a change once in a while too. Why don't we go to the mall this weekend and get you a new haircut?"

"Okay," Michelle agreed. "Thanks."

Aunt Becky hugged her lightly and got up from the couch. "Great. Wash up. We'll eat in about ten minutes."

Michelle wandered into the bathroom and washed her hands. Then she stared at herself in the mirror. She blew her bangs off her forehead.

I knew my clothes were boring. But I thought my *hair* was okay.

Michelle let out a long sigh. Changing from boring to cool was going to be a lot harder than she thought!

Chapter
4

 "What do you think?" Michelle asked Cassie and Mandy. They were hanging out on the playground before school the next day.

Michelle was wearing her new cool clothes. Before she left the house she'd shredded them even more. Now they were super-cool.

Michelle had also put on some fake tattoos—a bright blue lightning bolt above one wrist, and a little rose on the side of her neck.

She hoped the tattoos would take attention away from her boring hair until she could get it cut.

"Wow! What did your father say?" asked Cassie. "My mom would go crazy if I did that to my clothes."

"He doesn't know I wore this outfit to school," Michelle admitted. "He leaves for work really early. But he was kind of upset when he saw these clothes yesterday."

"I like them," Mandy said. "They are pretty weird, but . . . sort of cool. And I love the fake tattoos!"

Yes! Michelle thought.

"The clothes and the tattoos are the first steps in my plan not to be boring anymore," Michelle said. "When I get new comments in the slam book, they are going to say that I'm cool, cool, cool!"

"I still say those things in the slam book don't mean you're boring." Cassie said.

"But I don't want to be just *un*-boring. I want to be exciting!" Michelle explained.

Michelle's friends Lee and Jeff walked

toward them. Michelle stood up extra straight and tall. And she turned her head to make sure they would be able to see the tattoo on her neck.

She couldn't wait to hear what they would say.

"Hey, Michelle!" Lee cried.

Michelle started to grin. It's working already, she thought.

"See you in class," Lee continued. He didn't seem to notice Michelle's new clothes or her tattoos at all!

Neither did Jeff. He just waved as he and Lee headed toward the school building.

Michelle frowned. She'd expected her friends to be *amazed* by her new look.

They weren't.

"I can't believe Lee and Jeff didn't even notice anything different about me," Michelle complained.

"You see how they dress," Cassie joked. "They obviously don't pay any attention to clothes at all!"

"Hey, Loreen! Great outfit!" Michelle heard Jeff yell.

She spun around in time to see Loreen heading into school. Loreen had on cowboy boots with sparkly rhinestones, leggings, and an extra-big T-shirt from a rock concert.

"I thought they didn't notice clothes," Michelle muttered to Cassie.

Cassie just shrugged.

Heather Zimmerman, a girl from Michelle's class, wandered up to them.

Heather will definitely notice a difference, Michelle thought. She fluffed the fringe on the bottom of her shirt.

"Hi," Heather said. "Do any of you remember how long our essay is supposed to be? The one on our favorite animal."

"Two pages," Mandy told her. "I'm writing about giraffes."

"I'm writing about penguins. I love the way they walk," said Cassie.

"I'm still trying to decide," said Heather. "What are you writing about, Michelle?"

Michelle couldn't believe it. Heather hadn't said a word about her new cool clothes! Or her tattoos!

"I'm writing about my dog, Comet," Michelle answered.

"That's a good idea," Heather said. "Too bad I don't have a pet to write about. I'll see you guys in class."

"Bye," Cassie and Mandy called.

Heather turned around when she reached the double doors leading into the school. "Oh, Michelle," she called.

Finally, Michelle thought. Fi-nal-ly.

"Do you still have the slam book? I haven't seen it yet, and Kelly said you were the last one who had it," Heather said.

Oh, no! Michelle groaned to herself. I need more time before I pass the slam book on. I'm not nearly cool enough yet!

"I'll look," Michelle said. "But I think I gave it to someone already."

"Okay." Heather continued into the school.

"She didn't notice either," Michelle wailed. "What am I going to do?"

"You know Heather," Cassie said. "All she thinks about is school, school, school."

Maybe Cassie is right, Michelle thought. Maybe she'd get a bigger reaction from the other kids in her class. She sure hoped so.

For the rest of the day, Michelle waited for kids to notice her. But they treated her the same as ever.

What was wrong with them? she wondered. Couldn't they see she'd gone from boring to cool?

Or was she so uncool that it was impossible for her to be cool no matter *what* she did?

No, I just have to work harder, she decided. I'm sure there are lots of things I haven't tried. I just have to figure out what they are.

As soon as the last bell rang, Michelle

said good-bye to Cassie and Mandy. Then she rushed home and dashed up the stairs to her room.

If she wanted to be cool like Loreen, she had to come up with something else to try—and fast. She couldn't keep the slam book stashed away in her backpack forever!

I should do something with my hair next, Michelle thought. She didn't have time to wait until Aunt Becky could take her to get it cut.

Michelle figured *Young Sass* would have some suggestions. Michelle picked up the magazine from her desk and started to read.

When she reached an article called "Turn Your Hair from Dull to Wow!" she smiled. This is it! she thought. This will do it! This is something *no one* will be able to miss!

Michelle studied her new hair in the bathroom mirrors at school. It turned out great, she thought.

But her stomach gave a little flip-flop.

What if I'm wrong? What if everyone hates what I did to my hair? she thought. What if everyone laughs?

No, *Young Sass* said it was cool, Michelle reminded herself. So it was cool.

She took a deep breath and opened the bathroom door. Mrs. Yoshida's classroom was right around the corner.

Michelle held her head up, smiled like the *Young Sass* model, and strolled toward the classroom door, trying to look as cool and casual as possible.

"Your hair!" Mandy shouted when she spotted Michelle. "What happened?"

Cassie ran toward her, then stopped so suddenly, her sneakers squealed on the linoleum. "Oh, wow! Wow!" she cried. "Michelle, your hair . . . it's . . . it's blue!"

Chapter 5

♥ "Blue Kool-Aid," Michelle told her friends. "Maybe I'll try Strawberry Red tomorrow! I'm going to make my hair a different color every day. *That's* definitely not boring!"

Mandy circled her. "But your blond hair was so pretty," she said.

"I think blue is even prettier," Michelle answered. "Besides, it's my favorite color!"

"What does your family think?" Cassie asked.

"I wore a hat this morning," Michelle answered. "No one saw it."

"Well . . . your new hair *does* go with your new clothes," Mandy admitted.

Michelle wore her cut-up jeans with an old plaid shirt of Joey's. The shirt came down to her knees.

"I liked your old clothes better," Cassie muttered. "You don't even look like yourself."

"I know. Isn't it great?" Michelle asked. "Sometimes I can't believe how much I've changed in only a couple of days. And I still have something else to add to my look."

She reached into her pocket and pulled out a small silver clip-on nose ring. "Isn't it awesome?" She popped it onto her left nostril.

"Ow!" The nose ring pinched a little. But Michelle thought it was worth it.

"Where did you get *that* thing?" Mandy demanded.

"It was on D.J.'s dresser," Michelle explained. "It was part of her costume from

29

a skit she was in at college. But she won't mind that I borrowed it. She doesn't wear it."

"I don't like nose rings," Cassie said. "What if you sneeze? Gross!"

A couple of fifth-grade girls walked by. They didn't say anything to Michelle. And they didn't stare. But Michelle could tell they noticed her—as soon as they passed by, she heard one of them whisper, "Awesome."

They know what cool is, Michelle thought.

A couple of third-graders hurried past, and they *did* stare. They looked totally impressed.

This is so great! Michelle thought.

Jeff, Lee, and Anna Abdul, who was also in her class, turned the corner and headed toward Michelle.

What are they going to think of the brand-new me? she wondered. She felt her heart beating faster.

Anna's brown eyes opened wide.

"Whooaa," Lee gasped.

"Cassie! Mandy! Aren't you going to introduce me to your amazing new friend?" Jeff joked. "I've never met anyone with blue hair before."

Kelly joined the group. "Michelle, you got your nose pierced! It looks fantastic!"

She doesn't know it's a fake! Michelle thought.

Michelle couldn't stop grinning. It felt so good to be cool. At last all her hard work had paid off. Everyone was noticing the new Michelle. And they loved her!

I did it, she thought. I really, really did it.

Then Michelle spotted Loreen coming down the hall. Perfect timing, Michelle thought. She can see my new hair and my nose ring—and she can see this whole group of kids gathered around me.

Michelle knew if *Loreen* thought she was cool, then everyone in school would think she was cool too. This is the test, she told herself.

"Hi," Loreen said as she walked into class.

Hi! That's it? Michelle couldn't believe it.

Loreen didn't seem impressed. She didn't even seem to notice a difference.

"Let's go in," Mandy said.

Michelle followed her friends into class. She sat down at her desk and unzipped her backpack. Then she pulled out her math book.

She zipped the backpack up as fast as she could. She didn't want anyone to see the slam book.

The other kids are going to start asking where it is soon, Michelle thought. I can't keep it much longer.

But she couldn't give the slam book

to anyone yet. She wasn't ready. She wouldn't be ready until she found a way to show Loreen that she was cool.

What am I going to do? Michelle wondered. I'm running out of ways to make myself cool. I need a new idea. Fast!

Chapter

6

♥ "Michelle, you have to stop worrying about being cool—at least until the game is over," Cassie said.

"Yeah, we all have to concentrate if we're going to beat the Seagulls," Mandy reminded her.

"You're right," Michelle answered as they headed out to the softball field that afternoon. "I promise I won't think about anything but the game."

Michelle wanted to beat the Seagulls almost as much as she wanted to be cool. Her softball team, the Sparrows, had never beaten the Seagulls. And the Seagulls never let them forget it.

"We've been practicing really hard," Michelle said. "We can win today. I know it!"

When they reached the field, Michelle grabbed Cassie's arm. "Look over there," she said. She pointed behind the baseball diamond. "It's Loreen and a couple of her friends!"

"So?" Cassie said.

"So this is great!" Michelle said. "if Loreen sees that I'm the captain of a great softball team, maybe she'll think I'm cool. And if *she* thinks I'm cool, everyone will."

"Michelle, you promised to stop thinking about how to be cool until the game is over," Mandy complained.

"Okay, everyone, huddle up," Coach Green yelled from the Sparrows' dugout.

Michelle, Mandy, and Cassie joined the circle around the coach.

"When did you get that?" Coach Green cried. She stared at Michelle's nose ring.

Michelle tilted her chin up so everyone on the team could get a good look. "Today!" she bragged. She didn't tell them the nose ring was fake.

"Well, you have to take it out during the game," Coach Green said. 'No earrings *or* nose rings when we're on the field," she continued, gazing from girl to girl. "You could tear an earlobe or rip your nose."

Michelle hesitated. She didn't want to take out the ring—not in front of Loreen.

"Now, please, Michelle," the coach said. "And I promise not to say a word about your hair."

Thank goodness for that, Michelle thought. Mrs. Yoshida had plenty to say about her hair that morning! And she made Michelle promise to save her ripped clothes for after school.

Michelle couldn't disobey the coach. She

pulled off the nose ring and stuck it in her pocket.

At least she can't make me take off my hair, Michelle thought.

"The Seagulls are batting first," said Coach Green. "Michelle, you take first base."

After the coach assigned the rest of the positions, Michelle led her team in a cheer. "Seagulls, Seagulls, have you heard? The Sparrow is a winning bird!"

Then Michelle trotted out onto the field and pulled on her baseball mitt. Okay, she thought as the rest of the team took their positions. This is the day we beat the Seagulls.

Josie O'Hara came up to the plate. She was the captain of the Seagulls—and Michelle couldn't stand her.

Every time Josie's team beat the Sparrows, she would say something really mean to Michelle. Last game she said, "If the

Sparrows had a better captain, they might have a chance of winning once in a while!"

You're not getting past first base today, Josie, Michelle thought. You're not getting past me!

Michelle leaned forward. She focused her eyes on the bat. Which way would Josie hit the ball?

Bzzz!

A bee landed on Michelle's bangs.

She swatted it away.

Thunk!

Josie smacked the ball.

It sailed straight toward Michelle. "I've got it!" she yelled.

Bzzz! Bzzz! Bzzz!

The first bee came back—and two other bees came with it.

Michelle jerked her head away from them.

"Look alive, Michelle!" Coach Green yelled. "The ball's coming right to you!"

Michelle tried keep her eye on the ball. But the bees kept swarming around her.

Bzzz! Bzzz! Bzzz! Bzzz!

More bees joined the others.

Plop!

Michelle heard the ball land on the grass. She heard Josie's feet pounding toward her.

"Go, Josie, go!" the Seagulls yelled.

Oh, no! She's going to make it to first base, Michelle realized. I'm not going to get the ball in time!

Michelle swatted at the bees with both hands. She had to stop Josie!

She dropped to her knees and patted the ground around her. Where was the ball? Where *was* it?

She couldn't see anything with the bees flying in front of her face.

Josie ran past first base. "Bye, Michelle!" she called.

Michelle choked on the dust Josie stirred up.

"What are you doing?" Coach Green cried. "The ball is right in front of you, Michelle. Pick it up and throw it to second!"

"Come on, Michelle!" Cassie yelled.

Michelle wanted to get the ball. But there were too many bees!

"Throw it to third!" the coach yelled.

"What are you doing?" one of the outfielders cried. "She's making a home run!"

Michelle could feel bees crawling through her hair. She could feel their little legs on her scalp. She couldn't take it one more second. "Get them off me!" she screeched.

She sprang to her feet. She hopped from one foot to the other. She flapped her arms. But the bees wouldn't fly away.

"Throw it home!" Coach Green shouted.

Michelle bolted off the field. "Beeees!" she yelled.

She grabbed a water bottle from the bench and dumped it over her head.

"Yay!" the Seagulls yelled. "Home run!"

"Michelle, what's wrong?" Coach Green exclaimed.

"Bees! Bees! In my hair!" Michelle cried. "Are they gone?"

The coach gently ran her fingers through Michelle's wet hair. "They're gone," she said.

"Hey, Michelle," Josie called from the Seagulls' dugout. "Can you teach me that dance you were doing out on the field?"

Michelle started to answer—then she remembered Loreen.

She spun around. Loreen and her friends were standing in the bleachers. And they were laughing.

Chapter

7

♥ *Young Sass* should have said that bees love blue Kool-Aid, Michelle thought as she blow-dried her hair that afternoon.

It was back to its blah, blah, boring blond again. She'd washed the blue Kool-Aid out. She wanted to be cool—but not enough to get covered in bee stings!

What was she supposed to do? She'd planned to use Kool-Aid to change her hair color every day. That idea was definitely out now!

But she couldn't go to school with her old hair. That would be a step backward.

Michelle shut off the blow dryer and snapped her fingers. I know what to do! she thought.

She hurried out of her room and headed for the attic. But before she reached it, Nicky and Alex burst into the hall.

The twins ran up, and each of them hugged one of her legs. "Michelle! Michelle!" they chanted.

Michelle gave them both a big hug. "Hi, guys!" She loved spending time with Nicky and Alex. They were so cute!

"Color with me!" Nicky begged.

"No! Play Legos with me!" Alex cried.

"Later, later," Michelle promised. It made her feel good that the twins got so excited every time they saw her.

But she couldn't play with them now. She had important things to do.

Michelle hurried up to the attic and over to the big trunk where the Tanners kept all their old Halloween costumes. It's in here somewhere, Michelle thought.

She yanked open the lid and started rummaging through the trunk. She found some ballet tutus, an enormous pair of clown shoes, a Darth Vader helmet. No, no, no, she thought.

She found some glow-in-the-dark vampire fangs, a Raggedy Ann dress—and a black witch's wig. Yes!

Michelle grabbed the wig and stuffed everything else back in the trunk. Then she rushed down to her bedroom and hurried straight to her art box. Time to use her trusty scissors again!

She stuck the wig on and gave it a short, spiky cut. Then she sprayed on some mousse to make the top extra spiky.

She studied her newest look in her mirror. Pretty cool, she thought. But she knew her family would have a fit if they saw her wearing it.

Michelle took off her wig and tucked it

in her backpack. She would put the wig on in the morning, right before school.

Michelle ran her fingers through her spiky black hair. She sat at her usual lunch table, waiting for Cassie and Mandy. They were both buying their lunch today.

"We can't be in the talent show," Michelle heard a boy say behind her. "Brian broke his arm, and now we don't have anyone to play electric guitar."

"That's a bummer, Spike," another boy answered. "Do you know anyone else who can play?"

Spike! He must be talking about the talent-show act he's doing with Loreen.

Michelle turned around. "I can play electric guitar," she blurted out.

It's not really a lie. I can *learn* to play, she thought. Uncle Jesse can teach me.

She felt her heart beat faster. Don't blow it, she told herself. This is your big chance.

If she were in a rock band with Loreen, there would be no question about it. Kids would write in the slam book that she was awesome and amazing too. Michelle just knew it.

"You new in school?" Spike asked in a raspy voice. His friend wandered off.

Wow! Spike didn't even recognize her! He'd probably never even noticed her before.

"I've been here a while," Michelle replied, making her own voice raspy like Spike's. She was afraid if she told him who she was, he wouldn't want to talk to her.

Michelle ran her fingers through her spiky hair.

I used to be a dweeb, she thought. That's why you don't know who I am now.

Michelle loved having a new image. It was so much fun!

"Wait a minute," Spike said. "Your name is Michelle . . . something, right?"

Michelle. Suddenly it sounded so boring.

"It used to be," she told him. "Now it's Jet. Jet Tanner."

The name just popped out of her mouth. But it fit. It sounded like a cool person's name.

Spike nodded. "I know how that is. My name used to be Harold before I changed it. I *hate* the name Harold."

"Spike is *much* cooler," Michelle agreed.

"Hey, my dad is taking me and Loreen out for pizza tomorrow after school. We need to talk about the talent show. Want to come?" he asked.

"Great," said Michelle. She tried not to sound too excited. But she felt like spinning around the room.

Cassie and Mandy strolled over with their trays. "Later, Jet," Spike said.

"What did he call you?" Mandy asked as she sat down next to Michelle.

"Jet," Michelle said. It sounded just a little bit silly now. "It's my new name."

Cassie giggled. "What do you need a new name for?" she asked.

"To fit my new cool self," Michelle said.

"Maybe I should get a new name too," Cassie said. "Like . . . Ladybug."

"No, no. That's totally uncool. You need something like TurboGirl," Mandy said.

They both cracked up.

"It's not funny," Michelle said. "I told you I don't want to be boring anymore. I don't want anyone to think I'm *"not much"*—or any of those other things people wrote about me in the slam book."

"Hey, we wrote great stuff about you," Mandy said.

"That's different," Michelle muttered.

Why was it so hard to explain things to her two best friends lately?

"I'm sorry we laughed," Cassie said. "I know you want to show everyone how cool you are."

"Yeah, and it's easy to be boring if you have a boring name," Michelle said.

"Do you think *Cassie* is a boring name?" her friend asked.

Michelle didn't answer. She didn't want to hurt Cassie's feelings. But Cassie *was* a pretty lame name. The name Mandy wasn't too cool either.

"Guess what I got in the mail yesterday?" Mandy said. Michelle could tell she was trying to change the subject. "A two-for-one coupon from that ice cream shop where they put the ice cream in little silver bathtubs! My mom promised she would take us right after school tomorrow. She'll even pay for the ice cream."

"That sounds great!" Cassie exclaimed. "I bet I already know what Michelle—I mean Jet—is going to have. That chocolate sundae with cherry sauce, right?"

"Right," Michelle said. "I mean, that's what I would have—but I can't go tomorrow."

"Why not?" Cassie asked.

"Uh, I've got detention," Michelle lied. How could she tell them she'd rather do something with Spike and Loreen? She couldn't!

Michelle reached under her wig and scratched her scalp. It really itched. And the nose ring was pinching her nostril again.

"Detention? For what?" Mandy cried.

Michelle had to think fast. Was there any time she hadn't been with Cassie and Mandy today? Yes—when she went to the library.

"I got caught talking really loud in the library," Michelle told them.

"That's awful!" Cassie said.

"You don't deserve detention for that!" Mandy exclaimed.

They both looked so upset. They are great friends, Michelle thought.

She felt her stomach squeeze into a little

ball. They're really great friends—and I'm lying to them!

Is it worth lying to Cassie and Mandy so I can hang out with Spike and Loreen? Michelle thought.

Yes—Spike and Loreen were the coolest kids in school.

Besides, Cassie and Mandy would never find out the truth.

Chapter 8

♥ Look at me now! Michelle thought. It hasn't even been a week since I started trying to be cool. And here I am hanging out with the coolest kids in school!

Even Spike's dad was cool! He told her he loved her nose ring. Michelle couldn't imagine Cassie's or Mandy's father saying something like that. Michelle glanced around the pizza parlor, hoping some other kids from school were there. She wanted everyone to see her with Loreen and Spike.

She didn't see anyone. Oh, well, she

thought. It won't take much time for everyone to figure out I'm part of the cool group.

"Have you been playing electric guitar long, Jet?" Spike asked.

"Jet?" Loreen repeated. "You changed your name, Michelle?"

"Yeah," Spike answered before Michelle could open her mouth. "Much better, right?"

Loreen nodded.

"I kind of like the name Michelle," Spike's dad commented. "But I guess Jet is better for a rocker!"

"So how long have you been playing?" Loreen asked.

"Pretty long," Michelle said. She couldn't admit she didn't play at all!

"That's great!" Loreen exclaimed. "We really need someone to play for the talent contest. We have permission to practice in the cafeteria after school every day for the next three weeks—starting the day after tomorrow. We're going to be the best! And after the talent show we can even form a band!'' She smiled at Michelle.

Wow, Michelle thought. I'm going to be friends with Loreen West! We're going to be in a band together!

Wait. I don't even know how to play, Michelle reminded herself. I've got to learn. Uncle Jesse has to teach me as soon as I get home.

She didn't want to think about what would happen if Spike and Loreen found out she'd lied to them.

They won't find out, she told herself. I'll practice so hard, they'll think I've been playing for years!

Besides, I have to learn only one song for the talent show. I can learn everything else later.

But what about the Sparrows! she thought suddenly. There was no way Michelle could spend every day for the next three weeks practicing with the band.

Unless . . . unless she gave up softball.

Michelle felt her throat tighten a little. She couldn't imagine being off the Sparrows for good. She loved softball—and hanging out with her friends after the games.

And she'd been looking forward to finally beating the Seagulls this season. The whole team had been working hard for that, and Michelle thought they were ready.

"What do you think, Jet?" Spike asked.

"Huh?" Michelle looked up and found Loreen and Spike staring at her. "Think about what?" she asked. She felt her face turning red. How embarrassing! She hadn't been listening at all.

Spike shook his head. "About what our band should be called."

Michelle had to say something—but her mind was a total blank. I wish Loreen and Spike would stop staring at me, she thought.

Come on, she ordered herself. Don't just sit there. She glanced down and caught sight of the tattoo above her wrist.

"How about the Blue Lightning Bolts?" she asked.

"I love it!" Loreen cried. "Go, Jet!"

"Outrageous!" Spike agreed. He gave her a high five.

"Even I like it," Spike's dad joked.

Yes! Michelle thought. She felt a big grin stretching across her face. They like me! They think I'm cool too!

Then she saw something that made her gasp.

Cassie and Mandy walked through the door.

Michelle slumped down in her chair as low as she could. She grabbed a menu from the next table and propped it up in front of her face.

Where was the bathroom? Maybe she could make a dash for it. She frantically scanned the restaurant.

No! She would have to cross right in front of Cassie and Mandy to reach it.

"Jet!" Spike said. He plucked the menu out of her hands. "We have lots of stuff to figure out before the talent show. What do you think we should play?"

"Michelle!" Cassie cried.

Michelle squeezed her eyes shut. This is horrible, she thought.

She opened her eyes and saw Cassie and Mandy rushing toward her.

"What are you doing here?" Mandy demanded. "You said you had detention."

"What are *you* doing here?" Michelle asked. "You're supposed to be getting ice cream."

"We decided to wait until you can go with us," Cassie told her. "What's your excuse?"

"I'm sorry. I'm really, really sorry," Michelle told them. She didn't know what else to say.

"Whoa," Michelle heard Spike mutter.

Why did this have to happen in front of Loreen and Spike? Why? Why? Why?

"You don't think we're cool enough for you? That's it, right, Michelle?" Mandy asked. Then she grabbed Cassie's arm. "Let's go."

"Wait!" Michelle called after them.

But it was too late.

Cassie and Mandy turned around—and left the pizza parlor without looking back.

Chapter 9

♡ The next day at school, Michelle stared across the cafeteria at Cassie and Mandy. Should I go sit with them? she wondered.

They're my best friends. I have to at least try to talk to them, she decided.

Cassie and Mandy hadn't even looked at her during Mrs. Yoshida's class. What if she went up to them and they didn't talk to her? What if they pretended she wasn't even there?

Michelle started across the cafeteria. She felt as if she were moving in slow motion.

"Hey, Jet!" Heather Zimmerman called as she passed by. "Are you sure you don't have the slam book? No one can find it."

I may as well give it back now, Michelle thought. I'm as cool as I'm going to get!

"Let me check my backpack one more time," she said. She unzipped it and carefully searched inside. "You're right. I did have it. It got lost in all this junk."

She handed the notebook to Heather, then kept walking toward Cassie and Mandy's table. When she reached it, she sat down across from them.

"I'm sorry. I should have told you the truth," Michelle said in a rush. "Spike asked me to go out for pizza with him and Loreen before you guys told me about going for ice cream."

"So why didn't you just tell us that?" Mandy asked.

"I thought you'd be mad at me for not going with you," Michelle said.

"It was a lot worse walking into the

pizza parlor and seeing you there after you said you had detention," Mandy said.

Michelle pulled out her sandwich and unwrapped it. It was Danny's special spicy tuna salad—one of Michelle's favorites. She took a bite, but she hardly tasted it.

"Uh, there is something else I need to tell you," Michelle said. She swallowed hard. Her throat felt dry and itchy. This is going to be bad, she thought.

"I quit the Sparrows. I called Coach Green last night," Michelle announced.

"How could you do that? We need you, Michelle," Mandy cried.

"All that Kool-Aid must have soaked into your brain," Cassie yelled. "You love softball! You don't really want to quit, do you?"

"Yes, I do!" Michelle insisted.

"But why?" Cassie asked.

Michelle's head started itching. She wished she could tear off the black wig and throw it on the floor.

"I'm going to play electric guitar in the talent show with Loreen and Spike," Michelle explained. "Then we're going to try to get a band together. I need a lot of time to practice. Besides, playing electric guitar is a lot cooler than softball."

Uh-oh. I didn't mean to say *that,* Michelle thought.

"That's all you care about now!" Mandy exclaimed. "Being cool! Well, Jet may be cool—but I liked Michelle Tanner a lot better."

"Me too," Cassie said.

"You two are just jealous!" Michelle snapped.

"Jealous!" Cassie snorted. "Of what?"

"Jealous because I'm popular. Lots of kids at school are noticing me."

"They are noticing that you're *weird,*" Mandy said.

"I am not weird," Michelle answered. "I'm cool—which is something you two will never be."

"I don't want to be cool if it means acting the way you do, *Jet,*" Cassie replied.

"Let's get out of here, Cassie," Mandy said. They began to gather their stuff.

Michelle felt her stomach clench. They weren't really going to leave, were they? Michelle thought. They can't. The three of them did everything together. They couldn't just stop being friends, could they?

"No, wait," Michelle said. "I'm sorry. I didn't want to get into a fight. I came over here to apologize, but you guys made me mad. Can't we talk?"

"There's nothing to talk about," Cassie told her as she shoved her books into her backpack. "We're obviously not cool enough for you anymore. That's just how it is."

"No, it's not!" Michelle cried.

"Bye, Michelle," Mandy said, zipping her backpack.

"Oh, by the way," Cassie added. "In

case you've forgotten, you don't even play the guitar!"

Michelle watched her two best friends walk away from her.

Fine, Michelle thought. I don't need them anyway.

Loreen and Spike are my friends. And lots of other kids will want to be my friends—especially when they read all the great new things everyone is going to write on my slam-book page.

I'll have more friends than I need. I'll have more friends than I can count.

But deep down Michelle knew none of them would be the same as Cassie and Mandy. She couldn't imagine life without her two best friends.

Chapter 10

♥ Michelle sighed with relief as she reached her front door. It had been so hard spending the rest of the day pretending to be cool Jet Tanner. Pretending that she didn't care how Cassie and Mandy felt about her.

When she stepped into the house, she found Stephanie, Uncle Jesse, Aunt Becky, her father, and the twins gathered in the living room.

Alex gave a shrill shriek of terror. "A witch!" he screamed. "A witch!" He threw himself into Jesse's lap.

Nicky burst into tears.

"What's wrong?" Michelle exclaimed. She hurried to comfort the little boy. But he cried harder as she got closer to him.

Oh, no! Michelle suddenly realized she'd forgotten to take off her wig and nose ring. She yanked off the black wig.

"It's just me, guys," she told the twins. "I didn't mean to scare you."

But the little boys wouldn't even look at her.

"Nicky, Alex, it's Michelle. It's Michelle," she said. "I'm sorry I scared you. I'm really sorry."

Uncle Jesse scooped up Nicky. "I'll take them upstairs. Don't worry, Michelle. They'll be fine." He hurried away.

"I forgot I had the wig on," Michelle told her father and Aunt Becky.

Danny jumped up and rushed over to her. "Michelle, where did you get that . . . that . . . that thing in your nose?" he asked.

Michelle pulled it off. "It's a fake," she said.

"Thank goodness!" He sighed.

Aunt Becky stood up from the couch. "Michelle, what's going on?" she asked. "You look so different!"

"Everyone thought I was boring the old way." Michelle crossed her arms. "Even you thought so, Aunt Becky! You said I should get a different haircut."

"Oh, Michelle," Aunt Becky said. "I just thought you wanted a change, so I suggested a different haircut. Nothing big. I didn't think there was anything wrong with the way you looked before—you looked adorable."

"But I don't want to look adorable!" Michelle cried.

"What's wrong with adorable?" Danny asked. "Adorable is *adorable*. I love adorable!"

"Adorable is for babies. It's not cool," Michelle said. He didn't understand at all.

None of them did. "I'm cool now. Don't you get it? Cool, you know—not a big geek!"

"Maybe you're a little too cool," Stephanie said.

Michelle glared at her. Couldn't her own sister side with her? "Traitor," Michelle muttered.

Stephanie made a face at her.

"Michelle, that's enough!" Danny said. "I want you to tell me exactly what is going on here. Why are you all dressed up like this?"

"I told you! I got sick of being boring little goody-goody Michelle. So I turned myself into someone much more interesting."

"*Interesting* isn't the word I would use," Stephanie mumbled.

Michelle couldn't take this anymore. She had to get out of there. They didn't understand, and they never would.

Neither did Cassie and Mandy.

She spun around and dashed up the

stairs to her room. She yanked open the door and slammed it behind her.

Then she flopped down on her bed—right on top of the *Classy* and *Young Sass* magazines. She pulled them out from under herself and threw them across the room. A few seconds later she heard a knock on the door.

Her father came in and sat down on Stephanie's bed. "We need to talk."

Michelle shoved herself into a sitting position. "Do we have to?" she asked.

"Yes," said Danny. "I need to know what's going on with you."

"Nothing," Michelle mumbled. "I just wanted to be cool and popular. And it's working. All the really cool kids like me now."

"But you've always had lots of friends," Danny said.

"But they aren't the really cool kids," she answered, staring at the floor. "And that's who I want to hang out with. I'm tired of being boring, average Michelle. I want to be someone exciting."

"I don't think you can be exciting by imitating other people—even other people you think are *cool,*" Danny said. "Let me ask you something. Are Cassie and Mandy in the group of kids you think are cool?"

"No," she answered.

"Do you think they're boring?" Danny asked.

Michelle thought of all the fun times she'd had with her friends. "No," she admitted.

"I bet they don't think you're boring either," Danny said. "Do you have a better time with the cool kids than you do with them?" he asked.

"Yes!" Michelle insisted. "I like being cool. It's great!"

"You didn't look too happy when you came home," Danny said.

Michelle didn't answer.

"You think about it." Danny stood up. He left the room and shut the door.

Michelle flopped back on her bed. Her stomach twisted into a knot as she thought about the fight she had with Cassie and Mandy at lunch.

They said some really mean things to her. But she shouldn't have called them jealous. Or said they could never be cool.

I still want to be friends with them, Michelle thought. Maybe I should call and apologize for what I said. They can't stay mad at me forever—can they?

Michelle got up and hurried out to the hall phone. She dialed Mandy's number.

Mandy's mother answered.

"Hi, it's Michelle. Is Mandy home?" Michelle asked.

"Aren't you with the rest of the girls?" Mrs. Metz asked. "All the Sparrows went to watch a soccer game at the junior high school."

71

"Oh, right," Michelle said quickly. "I, um, I forgot. Thanks." She hung up.

Michelle's eyes stung, and she felt a lump in her throat. Her whole softball team had plans—and no one told her about them. Not even Cassie and Mandy.

You're not on the Sparrows anymore, Michelle reminded herself. But it didn't help much.

Michelle rubbed her eyes hard. She wasn't going to cry.

That's it, she thought. I'm not going to try to apologize to Cassie and Mandy again. If they want to be my friends, they can apologize to me.

Then I'll think about if I want to say yes or not!

I might be too busy having a great time with Spike and Loreen.

But first I have to learn to play my song for our first rehearsal.

The night before, Uncle Jesse and Aunt Becky had gone out to dinner. They didn't get back until late, so Michelle hadn't had the chance to ask him for guitar lessons.

I'll do it right now, she thought. She took the stairs to the third floor two at a time.

"Uncle Jesse!" she called. She burst through the door into Uncle Jesse and Aunt Becky's living room.

Nicky and Alex didn't race toward her the way they usually did. They stared at her, their blue eyes big and round.

"Hi, Nicky. Hi, Alex," Michelle said. She kept her voice soft and gentle.

They didn't answer. How long will it take them to run up and hug me the way they used to? she wondered.

"What's up?" Jesse asked. "You came through that door so fast, I thought someone was chasing you."

"I need you to teach me how to play the electric guitar!" Michelle cried.

"Well, we could use another musician in the Tanner family. Sure, I'll teach you.

When do you want to start?" Uncle Jesse asked.

"Right now!" Michelle exclaimed.

"Right now?" Jesse repeated.

"Pleeeze?" Michelle begged.

"Why not? I'm not doing anything. The guys can watch me give you your first lesson." He crossed over to the row of guitars he had hanging on his wall.

Jesse pulled the smallest guitar off the wall. "This is a good one for you," he said.

"But this one isn't electric, is it?" Michelle asked. "Can't I try that bright red one over there?"

"That one's broken," Uncle Jesse told her. "When you plug it into the amplifier, nothing happens." He handed the small guitar to her. "This is a good one to learn on,"

He took down a guitar for himself, and they sat down on the couch. The twins plopped down on the floor by Jesse's feet.

"The first thing I'm going to teach you is which string plays which note. Then I'll teach you a chord," Uncle Jesse explained.

"Wait," Michelle said. "How long is this going to take?"

"To learn a chord?" he asked. "Not too long."

"No, no, no," Michelle said. "Not a chord. A song. I need to be able to play 'Hop Until You Drop' right away. And I have to be able to play it great!"

"How soon is right away?" Jesse asked.

"For school tomorrow," Michelle answered.

"I'm sorry, Michelle," Uncle Jesse said. "But there is no way you'll be able to play anything by tomorrow!"

"What if I stay up all night and practice?" Michelle asked. "Then would I be able to play just that one song?"

"Sorry, Michelle," Uncle Jesse said. "It isn't enough time."

What am I going to do? Michelle thought.

Cassie and Mandy already hate me. And if I can't play the guitar for Loreen and Spike, I'm sure they'll hate me too.

Michelle felt tears sting her eyes. If I can't play for our practice session tomorrow, I won't have one friend left!

Chapter 11

♡ Michelle stared at herself in the mirror in the girls' bathroom the next morning. She was practicing her excuses. "Bummer," she whispered. "I guess it's broken. I won't be able to jam with you guys today."

She smiled at herself. It will work, she thought. My plan will work.

Last night Michelle had come up with a great idea. She asked Uncle Jesse if she could borrow the red electric guitar. The broken one. When she plugged it into the amplifier, nothing would happen. That's what he said.

Loreen and Spike will understand I can't play with a broken guitar, Michelle thought. Then I'll tell them that I have to save up enough money to buy a new one. And that will give me enough time to really learn to play.

Michelle nodded. Her plan was perfect.

The bell rang, and she headed to Mrs. Yoshida's class with the guitar strapped across her chest.

"Hey, Michelle, I mean Jet, have you seen the new comments you got in the slam book?" Kelly whispered as Michelle slid into her seat.

Michelle shook her head, and Kelly slipped her the notebook. This is it, Michelle thought. Now I'll know for sure what everyone thinks about the new me.

She took a deep breath and turned to her page in the slam book. She saw the nice things Mandy and Cassie had written about her. And the comments like "not much" that had made her feel so bad.

And below them—wow! A whole bunch of amazing new comments.

I never knew Michelle—I mean Jet—could be so cool. What a change!

The coolest kid in the class.

Loreen used to be coolest, but now Jet rules!

One of a kind!!!!

I did it! Michelle thought. I showed them all!

She shut the slam book and passed it back to Kelly. "Aren't you excited?" Kelly whispered.

"Yeah," Michelle whispered back. And she was—sort of. But not as excited as she'd expected to be.

You're just nervous about the guitar practice after school, Michelle told herself. Once that's over, you'll feel great!

Michelle couldn't wait to get her broken-guitar performance out of the way. But each hour passed so slowly. By the time the lunch bell rang, she felt as if she'd already been in school for three straight days.

She picked up her lunch bag and headed toward Cassie and Mandy. Then she froze. I'm not eating with them anymore, she remembered. We're not friends anymore.

I guess I can eat with Spike and Loreen, Michelle thought. No, that would make me too nervous. I wouldn't be able to think about anything but playing the guitar.

Michelle sat down at a table by herself. She couldn't help thinking that in just a few more hours she would be back in the cafeteria. And she would be telling her biggest lie yet.

Suddenly Michelle did not feel hungry at all. She felt sort of sick.

Michelle marched through the big double doors of the cafeteria after school. The sick feeling hadn't gone away.

Loreen, Spike, and a few of their friends stood at the front of the cafeteria.

You can do this, she told herself.

"Hey, Jet!" Spike called. "You ready to jam?"

"Definitely!" Michelle called back as she headed over to them.

"Plug in your guitar, and let's rock!" Loreen said.

Michelle looked down at the amplifier. She didn't even know where to plug the guitar in!

I should have asked Uncle Jesse, Michelle thought. Who will believe I can play if I can't even figure out how to work the amplifier?

She knelt down and studied the knobs and plugs on the amplifier. Should I just try to stick it in someplace? she wondered.

Michelle glanced around. Loreen and Spike were busy talking to their friends. I'll just pretend I tried to plug it in, she decided. She stood up quickly.

"B-bummer," Michelle stammered. "I

guess my guitar's broken. I won't be able to jam with you."

"Oh, no!" Loreen cried.

Michelle noticed Cassie and Mandy wander into the cafeteria. They stood in back, watching her. What are they doing here? she thought. But she didn't have time to worry about it then.

"What's the problem?" Spike asked.

"I plugged this thing in and—" Michelle started to say. Then she glanced at Cassie and Mandy.

I can't do this, she thought. I can't keep trying to impress Spike and Loreen by pretending to be someone completely different.

Michelle took a deep breath and turned to Spike and Loreen. "I can't play electric guitar," she told them.

"What?" Spike exclaimed.

"No way!" Loreen yelled.

"I wanted to be cool," she explained. "But I'm going back to being plain old Michelle. I like softball—and my regular hair. I don't want to pretend to be someone totally different."

"You mean this was just a big joke?" Loreen demanded.

"No," Michelle answered quickly. "I really thought I wanted to be Jet. But I don't. Maybe we can still be friends."

"No way!" Spike exclaimed. "I was friends with Jet. A cool girl who played guitar and had great hair. I don't want to be friends with Michelle Tanner. She's boring!"

"Let's just do our song without her," Loreen said.

"Yeah, get out of here, Michelle." Spike sounded disgusted.

"Sorry," Michelle muttered.

She ran down the steps and didn't stop running until she was outside the school.

"Michelle, wait!" Cassie called.

Michelle turned around. Cassie and Mandy ran up to her.

"What happened after you told Spike and Loreen you couldn't play?" Mandy asked. "We were standing too far away to hear—but they looked really mad."

"Nothing," Michelle said. She didn't feel like talking about it. "What were you doing there anyway?" she asked.

"Well, we know you can't play the guitar," Cassie said. 'So we wanted to see exactly what you were going to do."

"Um, besides, we have something to tell you," Mandy said. "We're sorry we walked off that day in the cafeteria. You *have* been acting strange lately, but we still want to be friends—if you want to be. We miss you."

"Yeah, we figure you're still our same friend Michelle under all the new clothes and hair and stuff—right?" Cassie asked. She patted the top of Michelle's spiky black wig.

Wow, Michelle thought. What great friends!

"I'm sorry too," Michelle said. "I shouldn't have called you jealous."

"So we're friends again?" Cassie asked.

"Friends again!" Michelle cheered.

"Hey, congratulations on the new comments in the slam book. You did it, Michelle!" Cassie said. "You got what you wanted!"

"Yeah," Michelle answered. "But Spike and Loreen got really mad when I told them I couldn't play the guitar. I told them I hoped we could still be friends—but they told me to get lost! They didn't want to hang out with the old boring Michelle."

"We told you four billion times, you're *not* boring, Michelle. It's their problem if they think you are!" Mandy said. "So now that you're out of the band, will you join the Sparrows again?" she asked.

"I want to. I want to be there when we finally beat the Seagulls," Michelle told her. "I'm going to call Coach Green as soon as I get home."

"Yay! Just remember not to wear your Kool-Aid hair on game days," Cassie teased.

Michelle laughed. "No more blue hair for me!" she exclaimed. "I figured out my own way to be cool—playing softball and hanging out with my two best friends!"

It doesn't matter if you live around the corner...
or around the world...
If you are a fan of Mary-Kate and Ashley Olsen,
you should be a member of

MARY-KATE + ASHLEY'S FUN CLUB™

Here's what you get:
Our Funzine™
An autographed color photo
Two black & white individual photos
A full size color poster
An official **Fun Club**™ membership card
A **Fun Club**™ school folder
Two special **Fun Club**™ surprises
A holiday card
Fun Club™ collectibles catalog
Plus a **Fun Club**™ box to keep everything in

To join Mary-Kate + Ashley's Fun Club™, fill out the form
below and send it along with

U.S. Residents – $17.00
Canadian Residents – $22 U.S. Funds
International Residents – $27 U.S. Funds

MARY-KATE + ASHLEY'S FUN CLUB™
859 HOLLYWOOD WAY, SUITE 275
BURBANK, CA 91505

NAME:_____

ADDRESS:_____

_CITY:_____ STATE:_____ ZIP:_____

PHONE:(____) _____ BIRTHDATE:_____

TM & © 1996 Dualstar Entertainment Group, Inc.

FULL HOUSE™
Michelle

#1: THE GREAT PET PROJECT 51905-0/$3.50

**#2: THE SUPER-DUPER SLEEPOVER PARTY
51906-9/$3.50**

#3: MY TWO BEST FRIENDS 52271-X/$3.99

#4: LUCKY, LUCKY DAY 52272-8/$3.50

#5: THE GHOST IN MY CLOSET 53573-0/$3.99

#6: BALLET SURPRISE 53574-9/$3.99

#7: MAJOR LEAGUE TROUBLE 53575-7/$3.99

#8: MY FOURTH-GRADE MESS 53576-5/$3.99

#9: BUNK 3, TEDDY, AND ME 56834-5/$3.99

**#10: MY BEST FRIEND IS A MOVIE STAR!
(Super Edition) 56835-3/$3.99**

#11: THE BIG TURKEY ESCAPE 56836-1/$3.99

#12: THE SUBSTITUTE TEACHER 00364-X/$3.99

#13: CALLING ALL PLANETS 00365-8/$3.50

#14: I'VE GOT A SECRET 00366-6/$3.99

#15: HOW TO BE COOL 00833-1/$3.99

A MINSTREL® BOOK

Published by Pocket Books

Simon & Schuster Mail Order Dept. BWB
200 Old Tappan Rd., Old Tappan, N.J. 07675

Please send me the books I have checked above. I am enclosing $_____ (please add $0.75 to cover the postage and handling for each order. Please add appropriate sales tax). Send check or money order--no cash or C.O.D.'s please. Allow up to six weeks for delivery. For purchase over $10.00 you may use VISA: card number, expiration date and customer signature must be included.

Name _____

Address _____

City _____ State/Zip _____

VISA Card # _____ Exp.Date _____

Signature _____

1033-19

FULL HOUSE™
Stephanie